Practical Instr
for Detecti
A Complete Course in Secret Service Study

Emmerson Wain Manning

Alpha Editions

This edition published in 2024

ISBN 9789361473296

Design and Setting By

Alpha Editions
www.alphaedis.com

Email - info@alphaedis.com

As per information held with us this book is in Public Domain.
This book is a reproduction of an important historical work.
Alpha Editions uses the best technology to reproduce historical work
in the same manner it was first published to preserve its original nature.
Any marks or number seen are left intentionally to preserve.

Contents

PREFACE	- 1 -
CHAPTER I	- 3 -
CHAPTER II	- 10 -
CHAPTER III	- 19 -
CHAPTER IV	- 21 -
CHAPTER V	- 29 -
CHAPTER VI	- 30 -
CHAPTER VII	- 32 -
CHAPTER VIII	- 38 -
CHAPTER IX	- 42 -
CHAPTER X	- 45 -
CHAPTER XI	- 47 -

PREFACE

Having been connected for many years with two of the largest and most successful private detective agencies in this country, both as an operator and as an official, and having been requested to outline briefly and concisely the most modern and up-to-date methods employed by leading detectives and private detective agencies of today, I shall confine myself in these pages to facts and a few personal experiences. I will endeavor to show that any person possessed of average intelligence, and who will use good common sense, can become a successful detective, regardless of his present or previous occupation.

This country today stands in need of more and better detectives than ever before in its history, and if one be inclined to doubt this statement he need only pick up the morning newspaper of any city of any size and be convinced that this is true. Hundreds of crimes of all descriptions are committed daily and statistics show that more than fifty per cent of persons committing crimes go unmolested and unpunished. Besides, there are the thousands of employees on our various transportation systems, in banks, stores, and in mercantile establishments, who are daily committing thefts of various kinds from their employers and whose nefarious operations are rarely uncovered, when one considers the actual number of thefts committed.

One may wonder why such conditions exist, or why so many criminals can operate without detection. It is because of the lack of sufficient trained detectives to hunt down the criminals and to ferret out the crimes.

It has been said that every criminal, no matter how careful he may be in his operations and regardless of the nature of his crime, will leave some trail or clue by which he may be detected. All good detectives will vouch for the truth of this statement. For the real detective no case is too complicated nor too difficult. More trained detectives are needed, and until we have them, undetected crimes and unpunished criminals will continue on the increase.

Every large city, every corporation, transportation company, mercantile establishment and manufacturing concern is constantly in need of detective service. There are thousands of concerns, also individuals, who are ever on the alert for the opportunity to employ good detectives. To the young man who may wish to connect himself with some reliable detective agency it will be well to keep in mind the following:

That when making application for such position he very likely will encounter such inquiries as: "What can you do?" or "What do you know about detective work?" In order to secure a position in any line it is essential that one have not only a talking knowledge, but also a working knowledge of the line. Careful study of what I shall set forth should enable any ambitious young man not only to secure a position as a private detective, but to "make good" as well; and if he so desires, to start and successfully conduct a private detective agency of his own.

DETECTIVE AGENCIES

With regard to starting a private detective agency, laws pertaining to the granting of licenses to individuals and companies to engage in such business vary in almost all of our states. In order to engage in the business, in some states it is necessary to secure and pay a business license, the rate per year being approximately the same as is paid by any other business concern. In some states licenses to engage in private detective work and to conduct private detective agencies are granted only by the courts of the county in which it is proposed to establish the main office or headquarters of the agency. Ability and fitness to hold such licenses must be established before the court granting them. This usually is accomplished by the applicant having several persons of responsibility vouch for his good character, fitness and ability. In some states bond must also be furnished to the state as a guaranty against misuse of the privilege that such license affords. Where such licenses must be secured I would advise that a reliable attorney be consulted.

It must not be construed that every private detective must have a license issued in his name or secured by him in order to operate in the state wherein licenses are required. In such states an agency must necessarily have a license, but as a rule agencies employ as many operators as they may require. Operators work under the licenses of the agencies that employ them. In starting a detective agency it is by no means necessary to engage a suite of elaborate offices. I have known many successful agencies to have been conducted from one or two modest office rooms, for which only nominal rentals were paid.

When starting an agency one of the first things to be done is to announce to business concerns, private persons, and the public in general the fact that the agency is open for business, at the same time advising of its location and how it may be communicated with by telephone and telegraph. Letters of announcement should be mailed direct to prospective clients whom it may be desired to reach.

CHAPTER I

SHADOWING

Shadowing, or more correctly speaking, keeping under surveillance some person, building or premises, is one of the most important branches of detective work. I know of many private and other cases wherein shadow work proved to be the only means of securing results. In my experience in handling and placing shadows, and in directing cases which necessitated shadow work, I have found that if one is to have any degree of success at shadowing, he should in the first place be a person not above medium height, of medium build, and preferably smooth shaven.

While at work the shadow should give out no intimation of being interested in what may be going on around him, although he should be at the same time alert and watchful and alive to everything that may transpire near him. The shadow should wear no conspicuous clothing, shoes or jewelry. Patience is the most important requisite to insure success in this branch of the work. While at work the shadow must never for an instant allow his attention to be detracted from the person or place he may be watching.

To my own discredit, I will relate how I once shadowed a woman for five weeks, hoping to be on hand when she would meet a certain person. I was purposely occupying at the time a room in a house across the street from where the woman lived, and from which point of vantage I was enabled to observe, unknown to her, when she left or entered the house. On the opportune night, when I should have been watchful and wide awake, I found, no doubt because of my long vigilance, that I had slept for ten or twelve minutes. Later I learned that the woman left her apartments during the few minutes that I had slept, and, with no intention on her part, gave me the slip.

In these days of fast trains, street cars, high powered automobiles and taxicabs, which offer swift means of travel, the detective when shadowing should be prepared at all times to cope with such conditions. He should ever keep in mind the fact that his subject, whether he or she be a criminal or not, is liable to travel in accordance with what his or her means will permit. On another page I will take up the matter of shadowing criminals, but will state here that the detective, unless he has had experience, should not undertake to shadow a person who may have reason to suspect being shadowed. It has been my experience that boys can accomplish the most when such persons are to be shadowed.

I have in mind a case where it was desired to have shadowed on a certain day, a woman who lived in an exclusive residential section of a large city. No man could have remained in the neighborhood in view of this woman's home longer than half an hour until he would have attracted the attention of every person in the block. For this particular case two young boys were selected to do the shadowing. They proceeded to a point near the woman's home, and apparently paying no attention to anyone, engaged in a game of marbles. When leaving her home the woman passed within a few feet of the boys and of course did not suspect their purpose. Three blocks distant the boys boarded the same car with her, and were thus enabled throughout the day to observe the woman's every movement, and without having attracted her attention at any time.

We will suppose that it is desired to keep under surveillance an employee of a bank, office or store. It is advisable in such cases that the person to be shadowed shall at no time see the detective if it can be so arranged. In my experience I have found that under most conditions the following plan will be most feasible for taking up surveillance of such persons. The plan applies also to any other occupants of such places. A detective other than the one who is to do the shadowing should visit the place where the person to be shadowed is located. When making such a call the detective may use the pretext of having called to solicit insurance, or he may use any other pretext that will be suitable and which will not arouse suspicion.

While making such a call the detective must make the best of his opportunity to scrutinize the subject closely, and should make mental note of any peculiarities of the subject. The color of the subject's hair should be noted; the shape of his ears, nose, etc. The detective should look for the hat rack, and according to the season of the year should endeavor to note the kind of hat, overcoat or coat the subject will wear when he or she leaves the building. Immediately after coming away from making his call upon the subject, the detective should convey to the one who will do the shadowing, a complete detailed description of the subject. Detectives should immediately write down such descriptions and should never trust them to memory. The reason for this will become apparent when the detective undertakes to pick out of five or six hundred, or possibly a thousand employees, some certain employee when he or she leaves a large factory or office building.

The detective who has seen and talked to the subject should remain near the logical exit from the building and when the subject comes out should designate him or her to the detective who will do the shadowing. Subject will then be shadowed by a person whom he or she has never seen, and whose purpose will probably not be suspected if noticed. Should the streets be crowded, the shadow, under ordinary circumstances, may keep quite close to the subject, but must at all times be governed by the number of pedestrians on the streets at the time as to how close to remain to the subject. The subject must not be lost sight of for an instant, as invariably, in private cases, clients expect to be advised of every movement of the person being shadowed. Therefore, should the subject stop in the street to talk to anyone, careful note should be made by the detective of such persons, so as to be able, at the end of the day's work, to render a detailed description of every person with whom the subject may have talked or associated.

Care must be exercised by the detective when subjects board street cars. The detective should always endeavor to secure a seat in back of, and on the same side of the car that the subject sits. For the detective to sit anywhere in front of, or opposite the subject in a street car or railway coach would give the subject an opportunity to study his face and features, and which must be avoided. I know of a great many cases, however, when detectives boldly sat beside their subjects in street cars and by so doing were enabled to read letters and papers in the hands of the subjects, and even to engage them in conversation.

When shadowing is being done in large cities, detectives must pay close attention and use the best judgment when subjects enter large office buildings or department stores. As to office buildings it is usually desired to know at what office a subject may call, and in order to ascertain this to a certainty it is necessary that the detective enter the same elevator with subject and leave it at the same floor that subject does. While the subject proceeds to the office he or she intends to visit, the detective may pretend to have gotten off at the wrong floor, or may busy himself scanning the names on the various office doors. In cases of emergency it may become necessary to make a "fake" call at some office in order not to attract the attention of the subject.

After having made note of the office that the subject has entered, the detective may take up a position on the street or the main floor of the building and await the reappearance of the subject. Should there be more exits from the building than the detective can properly cover he should endeavor to obtain assistance. When subjects enter large department stores, which may have from one to four entrances, it is of course essential that the detective keep in close proximity to the subject at all times, whether a man or a woman. If the subject stops to make a purchase, or to make inquiry at some counter, the detective should do likewise at some nearby counter so as not to attract the attention of floor walkers or sales clerks. Often it becomes necessary for the detective to make purchases, but it is better to do this than risk losing the subject.

I know of countless cases wherein it was desired to have women shadowed in order to learn of their actions during an evening, but because of their having visited department stores in the afternoon detectives lost them and were not on hand to observe their movements in the evening.

Occasions often arise when subjects visit theaters while under surveillance. Very often it is desired to know with whom subjects visit such places. When a subject purchases his or her ticket the detective should make it a point to be next in line at the box office so as to see or overhear the kind of ticket bought. If successful in learning this, the detective can ask for a ticket in the same section, but one or two rows behind the subject, or in any other location that will serve his purpose.

Should the subject have previously secured his or her ticket and if it is necessary for the detective to ascertain if the subject is alone while in the theater, he may have to purchase several tickets until he locates the seat occupied by the subject. If a man or woman enters a theater alone, it must not be taken for granted that he or she is enjoying the performance alone. I have known many prominent men and women to meet clandestinely in theaters, although they did not enter or leave the theaters together. This is usually brought about by the man purchasing two tickets one or two days ahead and sending one by mail or otherwise to the woman; then, on the appointed night, they can occupy adjoining seats without entering or leaving the theater together.

When subjects visit railway ticket offices the detective can easily arrange to be near enough to overhear the point of destination, and then if desired can purchase transportation to the same point. In cases where subjects board trains without stopping to purchase tickets, the detective, if he cannot learn the subject's point of destination from the gate man or through any other source, should be governed by the kind of train the subject boards. If the train be a local one it would be advisable to purchase a ticket to the end of the run and leave it at the station where the subject leaves it. If it be a through train and the destination of the subject is unknown, a ticket should be purchased or fare paid to the end of the first division; then, if necessary, to the end of the next division, and so on.

If it be desired to have a person kept under surveillance for any length of time, it is advisable that the detective secure lodging near the home of the subject. From there it will be possible to observe the subject going to and leaving his or her home. If practicable it is always best for the detective to remain off the streets and away from public view.

In the apprehension of criminals of all classes, records of private detective agencies and police departments in this and other countries show that in most cases more or less shadowing was resorted to in order to effect the arrest of the criminals, and also to establish their guilt. I know of a good many cases wherein careful and diligent shadowing was the only means by which "yeggs," "hold-up" men, pickpockets, store thieves and others were "caught in the act" or "caught with the goods on them," which in most cases is essential in order to insure convictions.

Some of the leading private detective agencies and most police departments in cities of any size, maintain and keep up, to a wonderful degree of perfection, photograph galleries which are commonly known as "rogues galleries," and in which are kept photographs of all known criminals, provided an opportunity has been had to photograph them or to secure pictures of them. Along with these photographs detailed descriptions of the criminals are kept, also what are known as criminal histories which show the date and place of any previous arrest, the nature of crime committed, method of operating, term of sentence, etc. After a criminal has once been photographed his picture usually is well circulated and retained indefinitely, regardless of whether he remains in or out of prison.

We will take for instance a pickpocket, who in detective vernacular is known as a "dip"; or a safe blower, who in the same vernacular is known as a "yegg." If he has been arrested or convicted at any time for one of these crimes his photograph very likely appears shortly afterwards in the rogues galleries throughout the country, it is reproduced on reward circulars and mailed broadcast over the country, or is shown in police and detective magazines published for the purpose. If, after serving a prison term, the criminal ventures to some large city, the chances are that he will not be there many days until he is "spotted" by some city or private detective, unless he is cautious and keeps under cover.

As a rule, when detectives see and recognize him, yet know of no crime that he may have recently committed, or of no charge that can be brought against him, they shadow him to ascertain where he "hangs out"; then endeavor to have him kept under constant surveillance. I might state here that in my opinion there are very few detectives or police chiefs used to dealing with criminals, who believe a criminal can or will reform. But regardless of this, it has been found by detectives long ago to be a good plan to keep track of the time of release of criminals from prison, and then to watch them closely until they may commit another crime.

I know of a good many cases where by this method detectives were enabled to catch their men in the act of committing a crime, or if they were not on hand or nearby when the crime was committed, as a result of their shadowing they knew just about where the criminal was at a given time and who would have been likely to commit such a crime; therefore they knew whom to look for. A good detective will make a study of the records of criminals and their methods of operating. It is a well known fact that every criminal has a distinctive manner of operating, and these distinctive features should be studied by detectives. Detectives should also make it a point to know, as far as possible, what known criminals are in their city at any time. Then if a store, warehouse, or residence is burglarized, if the picking of pockets becomes prevalent, or if a safe in a bank or office is blown, the wide awake detective can know from the nature of the crime, and the method employed, whom to confine his attentions to.

If for instance a safe has been dynamited, if feasible, arrangements should immediately be made to have all known safe blowers in the city shadowed. In this way criminals have often been caught in the act of either dividing their loot, or in disposing of it. Careful and systematic shadowing has also been the means of bringing to light the identity of many a thief who, until found out, enjoyed the utmost confidence of his employers.

I recall the case of a young man of good family who was a trusted employee of a certain large business concern. Sums of money ranging from ten to fifty dollars disappeared weekly from the firm's cash, the thefts having covered a period of about three months before the identity of the thief was established. Four persons had access to the firm's cash, and all were in turn shadowed from the time they left their respective homes in the morning until they retired at night. This plan of systematic shadowing developed the fact that the young man in question was the only one of the four possible guilty ones who was not leading an exemplary life, and in addition it was found that once a week he visited and made deposits at a certain bank while away from the office during the noon hour. Investigation at the bank developed that the young man was depositing each week more than the amount of his weekly salary.

Upon being shown detailed reports of his every movement for a period covering four weeks, and upon being questioned regarding his deposits at the bank, needless to say there was no difficulty in obtaining a confession from this young man.

I was once called upon to place under surveillance for two weeks a young man who lived in an exclusive residential section of a large city. It was not feasible to have the detective obtain a room in the neighborhood or "cover" of any kind, and to have had the detective stand on the street in this particular neighborhood would no doubt have exposed his purpose in a few hours. I made arrangements for the services of a uniformed messenger boy, provided him with a few novels to read, then had him sit under a tree on a lawn not far from the subject's home. In this way when the subject would leave his home to go into the city, the messenger boy would signal to the detective who was stationed some three blocks distant at a logical car station, and where the detective's presence did not attract attention. The messenger boy's real purpose was not suspected, and this surveillance was continued successfully for a period of two weeks.

When conditions are similar to those in the case just mentioned I frequently have provided the detective with a pair of field glasses which would be used from a room that the detective would rent.

I have handled many cases wherein it was desired to keep under surveillance persons who visited the city each day, but who lived in the suburbs, or in thinly settled outlying sections of the city. In such cases two detectives were used, one to remain out in the suburbs to observe the car or train that the subject would board, after which this detective would telephone to the other one, stationed in the city, the number of the car or train upon which the subject would arrive in the city. In this way the subject can easily be picked up and his movements covered during the day. Shadow work properly directed and properly executed never fails to bring good results.

CHAPTER II

BURGLARIES

Private detectives are frequently called upon to investigate burglaries of banks, offices, stores and residences. If the burglary has been committed in the city or in the country, or in a large or small town, the detective who investigates the case should proceed to the place as soon as circumstances will permit. If the burglary presents the appearance of having been perpetrated by outside parties, a thorough investigation should be made and nothing overlooked. I know of dozens of cases of burglary in small towns in which no results were secured because of the fact that only perfunctory investigations were made, and these were not conducted along proper lines. In cases of burglary, especially where safes or vaults have been dynamited or wrecked with nitroglycerine, the detective should conduct an investigation along the following lines:

Notes should be taken and a record made of the name of the bank, store, firm or individual suffering the loss; the date and hour that the crime was committed; date and hour discovered; by whom discovered; and a descriptive list should be made of all articles known to have been stolen. If the theft consisted of cash, the respective amounts of gold, silver or currency should be ascertained. If possible, secure the numbers of any missing bills. If papers, checks or negotiable notes or securities have been stolen, banks or other places where they are liable to be cashed should be notified promptly.

A careful investigation should be made as to how entrance was gained to the building. If a safe or vault has been blown or opened, note should be made of the name of its manufacturer, whether or not the safe or vault was old or new, whether equipped with double or single doors, whether opened by key or combination, and from whom it was purchased. Note should be made as to the kind of explosive used, or if tools were used. If holes were drilled it is important to ascertain the exact size, and if possible the kind of drill used. If other tools were used the detective should endeavor to establish their nature, which usually can be done from the marks left by their use.

Professional burglars nowadays do not travel from place to place with tools on their persons, because suspicion might be aroused or arrest invited for carrying them. They often purchase or steal their tools locally at some hardware store or blacksmith's shop a few hours before the time set for the burglary. The detective should endeavor to establish, at least to his own satisfaction, whether the burglary is the work of a professional or an amateur; also if any known burglars or "yeggs" live in the vicinity where the crime was committed. If so, their most recent movements should be traced and checked up. If possible, names should be secured of any persons who may have been seen loitering in the vicinity. If the names of such persons cannot be learned, detailed descriptions should be secured.

If the burglary has been committed in some small town, the hotel registers should be looked over and any doubtful persons investigated. Finger and foot prints and measurements should not be overlooked, providing any are found at the time of the burglary. Photographs should be made of finger prints and measurements made of foot prints. Professional burglars, or persons representing them, disguised as umbrella menders, peddlers or beggars, often visit and look over the place it is proposed to burglarize. Any such persons should be given consideration by the detective in the course of his investigation. Proprietors of nearby garages and livery stables and their employees should be seen and interviewed; also ticket agents and section hands on any nearby railroads. Conductors and crews of passenger and freight trains should be interviewed; also crews of street cars. If any known criminals likely to have committed such crime are believed to have been in the vicinity, their photographs should be shown to nearby residents and others. Should a photograph be identified, the detective will have something upon which to work.

When taking descriptions of criminals or of suspects, the following details should be embodied, if possible to secure them: Nationality; age, height, and weight; color of hair, color of eyes; build; complexion, whether smooth shaven, moustache or beard; moles, marks or scars; kind of clothing worn, including hat and shoes; whether or not the person walks or stands erect or stooped; any jewelry or lodge emblems worn, and whether he has the appearance of being a business person, a clerk, a mechanic, or a laborer.

In cases of thefts of jewelry, silverware, clothing, etc., from private residences the detective should first endeavor to establish to his own satisfaction whether or not the theft has been committed by an outside party, or by some member of the household. If it is believed that some member of the household is responsible, a servant for instance, such persons should be questioned closely regarding their movements, when they last saw or handled the stolen articles, if they knew of the existence or location of them, what they were doing and where they were about the time the theft must necessarily have been committed, etc. A descriptive list of the stolen articles should be made up, and if the same consists of jewelry, silverware, cut glass or clothing, pawnbrokers and proprietors of places where such articles would likely be disposed of should be seen and questioned. A descriptive list of the stolen articles should be left with the proprietors of such places and arrangements made to be notified promptly in case any of the stolen articles are offered for sale or appraisal.

I recall having investigated for a bank a case which was at first believed to have been one of burglary from the outside. The bank had in its employ a well educated foreigner, who was in charge of the bank's foreign department. In order to conduct the business of this department of the bank, he was permitted the use of five hundred dollars in cash, and for which amount he was of course always responsible to the bank. The "burglary" was discovered about 7:00 A. M. on a Sunday by the colored janitor when he came on duty to clean the banking rooms. The "burglary" having been committed in the foreign department, the foreign manager was among the first to be called to the bank. When he arrived he recalled that he had neglected the night before to lock into the vault a tin box in which he kept the five hundred dollars extended him by the bank. This box seemed to have been broken open during the night and was found lying on the floor empty by the janitor.

I was called into the case the following day, and a few minutes after arriving at the bank the foreign manager called me aside and told me he suspected the colored janitor, and that I would do well to confine my attention to him. He, however, could give me no plausible reason for suspecting the janitor, which fact caused me to become suspicious of the foreign manager. I then began an investigation as to how the "burglar" had gained entrance to the premises, and found that a large transom over a side door had been forced in, seemingly from the outside; also a wire fly screen covering the transom space had been forced loose, which would have permitted any ordinary sized person to then have gained entrance.

The transom was held rigid and in place by a heavy metal side fixture, and I still recall distinctly having wondered at the time how a person could have possibly exerted sufficient pressure or force against it from the outside to bend double the heavy metal side fixture, and to have accomplished it without attracting the attention of police or other persons. After studying the situation from all angles, I obtained a ladder and examined closely the ledge over which the "burglar" was believed to have climbed. Between the transom and the outer edge of the transom frame, where the fly screen was nailed, was a space perhaps six inches in width, and which space was thickly covered with dust. I examined it closely but failed to find any finger imprints, or any other marks that would necessarily have been made by a person climbing through the transom.

I became convinced that the foreign manager was guilty. He was the last person to leave the bank on the night of the robbery. It was quite plain to me then that before leaving the bank he broke open the tin box, appropriated its contents, then pulled down the transom from the inside and loosened the fly screen to make it appear that a burglar had entered from the outside. I brought my discovery to the attention of the officials of the bank, who agreed with me that no burglar had entered from the outside. I then took the foreign manager in hand and recounted to him how I believed that the entire matter had been planned and executed, that the same was all very clever with but one exception—that being that he had neglected to take into consideration the coating of dust on the ledge. I told him, in the presence of three officials of the bank, to turn over the stolen money, which he did, but he was not prosecuted and the case was given no publicity. In this, as in practically all cases, it will be seen that the criminal, no matter how carefully he plans his crime, usually leaves some clue by which he can be detected, and which clues, as a rule, can be developed by thorough investigation on the part of the detective.

By permission of the Current Literature Publishing Company, we quote from the May 1915 number of "Current Opinion" an article dealing with the technique of crime according to Inspector Cornelius F. Cahalane, a noted instructor of detectives, appointed to the metropolitan police force of New York:

"Practically every burglary is prearranged and the details planned. Burglars guard against the ordinary precautions which they think a live policeman will take to prevent their crimes or to capture them. Do not imagine that every burglar or thief wears a peak cap, box coat, sweater, striped trousers or bull-nosed shoes, so typical of stage burglars. They realize that to dress in such a manner would arouse immediate suspicion, and, accordingly, dress and carry themselves in a manner least likely to attract attention. They do not, as most persons fancy, carry burglary tools on their persons at all times. They know that it is not only a violation of the law, but that it is circumstantial evidence as well. Hence burglars carry tools no longer than is absolutely necessary. Sometimes they hide their tools near the scene of the contemplated burglary. If they have tools in their possession and think they are going to be searched, they will try to hide them or throw them away. Tools are carried frequently in musical instrument cases.

"There are many different types of burglars, who resort to various means in plying their calling. The burglars most dangerous to society are those known as 'Dutch house men.' They are the most desperate. They always work heavily armed and to accomplish their purpose or to avoid capture will take life under the slightest provocation. They usually operate in an inhabited dwelling, and to gain entrance, secrete themselves in some part of the building or grounds until they think the occupants have retired;

then, if necessary, they make their way to a roof, fire-escape or porch, and get in by prying open a skylight or jimmying a window sash.

"As a rule, householders fasten windows leading to fire-escapes or porches, but are careless about the other windows. 'Dutch house men' know this failing and often take advantage of it. They fasten one end of a rope (which one of them may have carried wound around his body) to a chimney on the roof and drop the other end over the ledge. One of them will lower himself to the desired window, open it and enter. They generally seek the place where it is most likely that valuables have been left before the owner retired, such as the tops of dressers or the pockets of clothing. In going from room to room, they usually place some obstruction, a table or a chair, in such a position that if the occupant should awaken and attempt to leave the room, he would trip over the object and make enough noise to warn the burglar that his presence had become known. Unless they are sure that no alarm has been given, they will seldom leave by way of the street; usually they secrete themselves on the roof or in the back yard and remain until there is an opportunity to escape.

"Flat thieves are not as desperate as the ordinary run of burglars, but they are burglars too, and they manage to steal considerable property. As a rule they will not enter an apartment while anyone is at home. They profit by the knowledge that housekeepers generally hide their money and valuables in a nook where they think a thief will be least likely to look—under rugs, legs of tables, under mattresses and beds, in sewing machine drawers, and the like.

"A flat thief requires only about five minutes in an ordinary flat, and when he is through it looks as though an earthquake had shaken the building. He starts by pushing the furniture to one end of the room. He turns the rugs over, empties the contents of bureau drawers into the middle of the floor, where they are examined, throws mattresses to the floor, cuts them open if he has not already discovered the hiding place, turns vases and bric-a-brac upside down, and, in this way, has every part of the flat searched in a short time. Flat thieves are usually young men between the ages of sixteen and thirty years.

"They gain entrance by ringing the vestibule bells, and, if no response is made, they assume that no one is at home, and enter the hallway and proceed to the apartment selected. If the door is locked they either use a false key or jimmy it open. Or, they may watch persons leaving their apartment, and enter during their short absence. If questioned, they try to represent themselves as peddlers, agents, inspectors of telephones, gas, water or electricity, or mechanics. They usually bundle together the proceeds of a theft and carry it to the street, passing through the halls with an air of bravado, so as not to excite suspicion. They generally work in pairs; one standing in the hallway to warn his partner of the return of the tenant, and, in case the thief is pursued, to trip the person in pursuit or to divert him in some other way. They seldom leave a house together, but usually meet at a distance from the scene to dispose of the property and divide the proceeds.

"Many flat thieves work by hiring a room or rooms in a residential section of the city and as near the roof as possible, particularly where the roofs in the vicinity are of about the same height. They use scuttles and fire-escapes as a means of getting into buildings and convey the plunder over the roofs to their rooms. In this way they avoid the danger of being detected in the street.

"More ambitious than the flat thief, but in something of the same class, is the loft burglar. Loft burglars are the most feared by merchants, for when they make a haul it is usually a big one, amounting to thousands of dollars. They are necessarily the brainiest of burglars for the reason that their work requires more and better planning. Plans are often made weeks in advance.

"A loft is selected after a study of the location and the quantity and quality of the stock carried in it. Weeks are then spent in becoming familiar with the habits of persons who might be in a position to thwart or discover them, particularly the watchmen and patrolmen on post, and the customary time of opening and closing the building, noting the person to whom this duty is entrusted.

"A Saturday afternoon or night is generally selected for the entry. Sometimes it is necessary to gain entrance through a building three or four doors away and clamber back over the roofs. When the loft selected is reached they do not hesitate to cut through a wall to get one of their number in it; if necessary they will drill through the floor from the loft below or through the ceiling from the one above, lowering the first man down with a rope. The door of the loft is then opened from the inside if the circumstances warrant it. The loot is carefully selected from the most valuable stock. Packing cases are constructed from material lying about, filled, and nailed shut.

"They are now confronted with the most difficult task, that of getting the packing cases from the building. The property is seldom moved at night. They fear that the appearance of a vehicle at an unusual hour in a section of the city where lofts are located would arouse suspicion. Instead, if as a result of their previous study, they know that the loft will be opened at 7:30 A. M., a vehicle will be brought to the front of the building at about 7:20 A. M., the door opened from the inside by one of the gang dressed as a porter, and in the most bold and daring manner the cases will be loaded on the wagon. One of the gang may even engage the patrolman on post in conversation, possibly within sight of their activities. The bogus porters, if the circumstances necessitate it, will go back into the building and escape by way of the roof or through an adjoining building.

"Safe burglars know as a rule the particular make of each safe on which they intend to operate. Like loft burglars they plan far in advance and come prepared to break through any part of a building in order to get to the safe. They have been known, when working in an exposed position, to make a pasteboard safe, paint it to imitate the original, shove the genuine safe into an inner room and leave the substitute in its place. Others do not resort to this subterfuge, but simply bodily shove the safe into a position where they can not be observed from the street and begin operations. They try not to use explosives. The easiest way, the combination, is tried first. If this fails, the weakest part, the bottom or back, is tried. The ordinary safe is turned upside down and the bottom or back is cut out with a tool they call a 'can opener.' If the bottom or back resists, they drill a hole near the combinations and try to disturb the tumblers sufficiently to turn the lock. As a last resort a hole is drilled and charged with explosive. To deaden the report the safe is wrapped with material found on the premises or with blankets brought along. A lookout is usually stationed on the outside to signal in the event of peril. Safe burglars, like burglars who break windows or side lights, wait for the rumble of a passing vehicle to deaden the sound of an explosion.

"Store burglars generally gain entrance through a rear or side window. They travel in gangs of two or three, one always on guard, and steal from the till, cash register or small safes. They, too, have their work planned in advance, and know just what to do when they enter. The loot is seldom removed through the front of the building; it is carried through the rear yards or over the roofs of an adjoining building and thence to the street.

"If the booty is too bulky to transport on their persons, a push cart is hired or stolen for the purpose, or a milk or baker's wagon is pressed into service, sometimes with the consent of the driver, and the goods moved early in the morning, during the hours when milkmen and bakers are making their deliveries, so as not to excite suspicion. Burglars who break store windows and side lights work in pairs and are very tricky. Their outfit in most instances consists of a long piece of heavy wire and a heavy piece of cloth, such as part of a bed comforter, which they carry wrapped about their bodies.

"A store is selected which displays articles of some value in its windows. The habits of the man on post are learned, and at an opportune moment during his absence they will throw a padded brick or iron through the window or side light, having first placed the comforter on the stoop or walk to catch the broken glass and deaden the sound. Or, they may use a glass cutter to remove a section of the window. This step accomplished, they dart into a nearby hallway and wait to see if the breaking of the glass has attracted attention. If they find it has not, operations are resumed and the contents of the show-window extracted by means of a stiff wire, the tip of which has been bent into a hook. The store selected is often covered by the crooks for hours, sometimes from an adjoining precinct or post, awaiting a suitable opportunity.

"The sharpest and most successful burglars of late have been foreigners, some of whom can not speak English. Their favorite method is to select a residence along some street-car route, enter it during the daytime, if possible, and remain secreted in areaways, back yards or on roofs until night, then force an entrance through a window, door or roof scuttle when the occupants have retired. After securing the plunder they open the front door and wait inside until a car passes. Then they run out and board a moving car, watching meanwhile to see if they are pursued. Sometimes they ride almost to the city line before getting off. They are afraid that if they pass a brightly lighted street corner they will be observed and for this reason they use the street cars.

"If there were no receivers of stolen goods there would be but little burglary of these or any other kinds: A thief will not steal unless he knows that he can make some profitable disposition of his haul. It is comparatively easy to dispose of jewelry, but a thief must know positively where he can immediately dispose of bulky property that he cannot readily conceal. Usually such stuff is immediately sold to unscrupulous dealers who carry goods of the same kind in stock; for instance, a quantity of stolen cloth may be sold to a dishonest dry-goods merchant. In some cases, however, a store or flat is rented in advance of a burglary or theft and the loot stored in it. The receivers are then visited in turn by the thieves, shown samples, and bids are requested. In this way they dispose of the goods more profitably.

"A careful thief destroys, as soon as possible, all marks of identification, but if he has not done so, the receiver takes that precaution as soon as the stolen property comes into his possession. Merchandise handled under unusual conditions should immediately suggest 'receivers' to you. For instance, if you saw a large quantity of silk being taken into a small retail store, or saw the delivery being made from a hand-truck or from a wagon not ordinarily used for such deliveries, or by persons who, from their appearance and manner of handling the merchandise, did not seem to be engaged in the business; or if you observed boxes of shoes being taken into a barber shop, or a great quantity of food being delivered to a dwelling, it should arouse your suspicion.

"Remember that persons engaged in a legitimate business are constantly devising ways and means of advertising themselves. They want everyone to know that they are engaged in a certain business, and located at a certain place, and invite inspection of their stock. They do not paint their windows to hide the contents of their store, or arrange the interior so that the stock will not be in plain sight, or deny prospective purchasers the privilege of examining their stock."

CHAPTER III

IDENTIFICATION OF CRIMINALS

In all up-to-date police and detective bureaus the Bertillon System is now being used whenever practicable for the identification of criminals. I consider it important that detectives be thoroughly familiar with the system, as it is a wonderfully accurate system of identification and quite easy for anyone to become familiar with, as I will show.

The Bertillon System of identification was unknown previous to the year 1880, in which year it was adopted in France as a standard by the police department of Paris, where it was introduced by Alphonse Bertillon, its founder. Since then it has been adopted by police departments of practically all large cities in the United States, Canada and Europe. For the identification of criminals the Bertillon System depends upon accurate measurements of various parts of the human body, having to do especially with the bones, which in adults never change. The parts measured are head, left ear, left foot, left middle finger, extended left forearm, outstretched arms, the trunk and height.

In the Bertillon System the metric measurement is used exclusively. In such measurement we have the meter, which equals 39.37 inches; the centimeter, which is the one-hundredth part of a meter and which equals 0.3937 of an inch; and the millimeter, which is the one-thousandth part of a meter and which equals 0.03937 of an inch.

In order to take the measurements of a criminal in accordance with the Bertillon System it is of course necessary to have and use a metric measure; one can be purchased almost anywhere in the United States for fifty cents. So as to make the matter of measurement more clear, I might state that under our own system of measurement we measure by yards, feet and inches, half inches, quarter inches, etc. Under the metric system we measure by meters, centimeters and millimeters. It will readily be seen that with the metric system it is possible to measure accurately the thousandth part of an inch.

We will take for instance a criminal whose height is five feet and one inch. In Bertillon or metric measurement his height would be one meter and fifty-five centimeters; written thus: 1 M. 55. 0. If a criminal's height be, for instance, five feet seven and a half inches, it would be, according to Bertillon or metric measurement, one meter, 71 centimeters, and five millimeters, written thus: 1 M. 71. 5. A criminal whose height is five feet and 7/8 inches would be shown in Bertillon in the following manner, with other measurements added:

1.67.6   1.74.0   88.1   19.0   16.0   14.5   6.0   26.1   11.8   8.9   45.4

HGT   OA   TR   HL   HW   CW   RE   LF   LMF   LLF   FA

These abbreviations signify, in the order shown, that this criminal's height is one meter, sixty-seven centimeters and six millimeters; outer arms one meter, seventy-four centimeters; trunk eighty-eight centimeters and one millimeter; head length nineteen centimeters; head width, sixteen centimeters; cheek width fourteen centimeters and five millimeters; right ear six centimeters; left foot twenty-six centimeters and one millimeter; left middle finger eleven centimeters and eight millimeters; left little finger eight centimeters and nine millimeters; forearm forty-five centimeters and four millimeters. The foregoing abbreviations have been adopted for convenience upon the backs of criminal photographs and where space usually is limited.

CHAPTER IV

FORGERIES

Although not generally known it is a fact that banks, business concerns, and the public in general probably suffer a greater loss through the operations of forgers and bogus check operators than through any other form of crimes perpetrated against them. There are confined today in the penal institutions of this country, thousands of persons convicted and found guilty of these offenses, and yet I would venture to state that not over forty per cent of this class of criminal is ever apprehended.

There is hardly a morning anywhere but what one may pick up a newspaper and read an account of how some clever forger succeeded in victimizing a bank, hotel or merchant. With this large number of forgers at large and free to operate when, and practically wherever they please, we have additional proof that there are today by no means sufficient trained detectives to run them down. The methods most commonly practiced by forgers, both professional and amateur, are quite well known, yet I believe it will be well for me to dwell at some length on the subject.

In a general way I might state that the methods of all forgers are much the same; at any rate such has been my experience with this class of criminal. Their aim in most cases, before presenting for payment a check to which a signature has been forged, or an endorsement, is to ascertain if the firm or person against whom the check is to be drawn has deposits sufficient to cover the check. After satisfying himself on this point the forger proceeds to fill in the check and to affix thereto a signature or an endorsement purported to be genuine.

After having selected the person whose signature or endorsement is to be forged, the forger must next be familiar with the handwriting of that person. It is comparatively an easy matter for anyone so inclined to secure an original, facsimile or tracing of the average business or professional man's signature. After providing himself thus the forger sets about writing a check that will be so near like the genuine that it will not be likely to be questioned when presented at the bank. The forger usually makes it a point to present his check at a time when the cashier or paying teller is busiest, and when the forgery will most likely pass unnoticed.

In my experience I have found that employers very often are careless in leaving their private check books, and sometimes signed checks, lying around the office where a dishonest employee or other person may have easy access to same. Very often cancelled checks fall into the hands of forgers who promptly take advantage of the handwritings for their ulterior purposes. There are dozens of ways by which a forger may secure them. Workmen who receive their salaries from their employers in the form of checks often are tempted to make use of the signature to forge others and have them cashed.

Under this class of criminal we have also to contend with what are known as bogus check operators, who, when writing and passing checks, use fictitious names of banks and persons; also the worthless check operator, who, after gaining the confidence of his employer, or of some bank, writes and has cashed a check in excess of funds he may have on deposit. The detective must not confuse forged checks with bogus checks. The former is a check upon which is written what purports to be the genuine signature or endorsement of some person and which signature or endorsement was not written by, nor authorized by that person. The latter is one upon which is written the name of some bank which does not exist, or which may be drawn on a bank which does exist but at which bank the drawer of the check has no account. There are also many other forms of checks passed which come under the classification of bogus checks.

Thousands of hotel keepers and merchants are victimized yearly through cashing forged, bogus and worthless checks presented by oily tongued swindlers who tell plausible stories as to how they happen to be out of funds, etc. In order to be successful in handling forgery cases it is essential that the detective be a good judge of human nature and of handwriting. The more technical knowledge he may have of handwriting the better.

If the detective is called upon to investigate, for instance, a case wherein a bank has been defrauded through the operations of a forger, he should endeavor first to see the forged check. A record should be made as to the kind of blank form the check was drawn on, whether or not same was drawn upon an ordinary counter check form, if the form was taken from a private printed check book, or from a pocket check book. Record should be made of the date, the number, on what bank drawn on, in whose favor drawn, the amount, how signed, and how endorsed. Such records should include whether or not the check or any part of it was filled in with pen and ink, with pencil, or with a typewriter.

For the detective's future reference a tracing should be made of all handwritings on the check, especially of any known to have been written by the forger. By far the best plan is to have both sides of the check photographed. Until such time as it may be needed as evidence in court, a forged check should never be taken away from a bank, carried in the pocket, or handled any more than may be absolutely necessary. The reasons are that in taking such a check from a bank it may become lost, and by carrying it or handling it the writings may become effaced. No chances should be taken in losing or destroying the most important evidence with which to prosecute the forger in case he is apprehended. The detective should place his initials or some other mark upon the original check so that he can positively identify it later if called upon to do so.

At the bank the detective should secure as thorough a description as possible of the person for whom the check was cashed, also should make note of any statements made by the forger as to where he came from, what firm he claimed to represent, or by whom employed, etc. Hotel registers should be examined closely for any registration in handwriting identical with that in the forged check. In order to establish the identity of the forger if not known, or to learn the direction in which he may have gone, the detective may proceed along the lines outlined with regard to burglary cases.

I have handled hundreds of forgery cases and will say that I never found the forger a criminal difficult to apprehend. There are two good reasons why this should be so; the first is that the forger, as a rule, must present himself in person at the bank or other place to secure the money on his check, and by so doing enables the detective to secure a good description of him, how he was dressed, etc.; the second reason is that the forger when filling in his check, or by endorsing it, must necessarily leave behind one of the very best clues for the detection of any criminal, that being his handwriting.

In fully ninety per cent of forgery cases I have handled I have found that the person whose signature was forged could tell, after being questioned, who was responsible for the forgery, and I will show you that the process is very simple and easy. I have in mind a good many cases each of which I cleared up in less than half an hour after arriving upon the ground. My plan was to first secure the best description obtainable of the forger, then a specimen of his handwriting, after which I would see or call upon the person whose signature was forged. To that person I would submit the description and the handwriting, and, as previously stated, ninety per cent of them were able to tell very quickly which employee, relative, friend, acquaintance, or enemy was responsible.

After the detective has learned the identity of a forger but cannot locate him, he should keep in touch, under some good pretext, with the forger's parents, wife, sweetheart, sister, brother or other relative or friend. The forger will communicate with his sweetheart, friends or relatives sooner or later; it is human nature and I have never seen it fail. When the detective has succeeded in causing the arrest of a forger, or of a suspected forger, he should endeavor to secure a confession from him. I have secured many confessions from forgers by saying to them in a friendly way that the best way for them to prove that they had nothing to do with the forgery with which they were charged, was to write a specimen of the forged check. It is really surprising how many professional forgers will allow themselves to be led into this simple ruse.

While the forger's mind is laboring under the strain of being under arrest, and seeing possible conviction ahead, he is eager to take advantage of what he thinks is an opportunity to prove that he did not write the forgery and will rely upon his ability to disguise his handwriting sufficiently to mislead the detective. Another reason why he will comply with such a request is that he will fear his refusal to give a specimen of his handwriting will be taken as an evidence of guilt. As a matter of fact I have found no persons in my experience who could successfully disguise their handwriting with their minds under any kind of strain. The forger can therefore be easily led into hanging himself with his own rope, as it were.

After securing such handwriting the detective should take out his facsimile, or photographic copy of the forged check, and if he finds the handwritings identical, he should point out the similarities to the forger. There should be no difficulty experienced in securing a full confession, and in addition the detective will have in his possession the handwriting of the forger, which, I neglected to state, should be secured in the presence of one or two reliable witnesses, so that the confession and handwritings can be substantiated in court if necessary. It goes without saying that efforts should be made by the detective to secure such handwritings and the confession as soon after the forger's arrest as possible. Should the forger or suspect have an opportunity to confer with an attorney before this is done, the chances are that no handwritings or confession will be secured.

Great care must be exercised by the detective when it is left to him to have warrants issued for criminals of this class. It often happens that one person will forge a signature or endorsement to a check, then delegate a confederate or other person to present the check for payment. Under these circumstances the presenter of such a check could hardly be convicted of forgery, but he could be convicted of passing the forged check and of obtaining money thereon. The point to be borne in mind by the detective in such cases is, that in order to convict a person of forgery, it is necessary to prove the handwriting, or produce one or more witnesses who actually saw the signature or endorsement being written. Warrants should be issued accordingly; the best kind of warrant to be gotten out in such cases being one in which the offender is charged with passing the forged check and with obtaining the money.

I have known quite a few clever forgers, who with the aid of good attorneys, succeeded in beating their cases simply because the warrants for their arrest were not properly gotten out, and which resulted in improper indictments being returned against them. I have known dozens of bungling detectives and officers to swear out warrants charging persons with forgery when, as a matter of fact, the forgery could not be proven, but a charge of passing a forged check and obtaining money thereon could have been made and proven. In the cases I have in mind the offenders went scott free simply because the wrong charge was brought against them, and because they were given advantage of the law itself to escape punishment.

As a whole I consider the forger one of the most dangerous of criminals to be at large, but as stated, one of the easiest to apprehend when proper methods are applied. I believe I will do well to recount here what I considered, when it was first submitted to me, my most difficult forgery case, but which in the end proved quite easy to unravel and clear up. One day it was discovered by a bank in a small town in the West that during the preceding seven months it cashed for some unknown person eleven checks to which were forged the signature and endorsements of one of the bank's customers. These forgeries were discovered when the customer came into the town from his ranch to have his pass book balanced. Upon being handed his cancelled checks he discovered the forgeries.

In this particular case no person connected with the bank could recall in the slightest degree for whom, nor for what kind of person they cashed the checks. From the fact that the customer called at the bank so rarely they did not know him by sight. Inasmuch as this customer lived far out from the city on a ranch, he could throw no light on who forged his signature to obtain the money from the bank, which, as I recall it, amounted to several hundred dollars.

In looking over the forgeries and the dates upon which they were paid, I found that they had been presented at the bank and were paid, on an average, of one every three weeks. Outside of the forger's handwriting, there was absolutely no clue upon which to work. After giving the case several hours' thought, I came to the conclusion that the case, to my way of thinking at that time, could be cleared up along only one line, that being that I find the person through his handwriting.

The town in question was a county seat of about five thousand population. I had concluded also that the culprit, from the fact of his forgeries covering a period of seven months, must be a resident, or at least an habitue of the town. I found myself figuring how long it would take to enable me to see a specimen of the handwriting of every man in the town. This being my plan I started to work along the line of least resistance, going first to the court house, where I secured permission to look over any and all kinds of records, in the hope of finding somewhere in the town a specimen of handwriting identical with that of the forger in the case. Near the close of the second day my search was rewarded through my finding upon the payrolls of a contractor a signature, every letter of which was identical with the same letter in the forgeries, the forger being at that time in the employ of the contractor. The same characteristics and peculiarities being evident in both handwritings, I lost no time in effecting arrangements for having the suspect brought before the town marshal and me.

We handed the man pen and ink and check forms, and upon his signifying his willingness to write for us specimens of any checks we desired, we of course had him write copies of the forgeries. His handwriting proved to be identical to the smallest detail, with the handwriting in the forgeries, and upon being shown both writings he made a confession on the spot. Later he pleaded guilty to the charge of forgery and was sentenced to serve two years in state prison.

A favorite method of offenders in defrauding banks, and which scheme is worked somewhere every business day of the year, is to visit a bank and open an account by depositing a bogus or worthless check, and which transaction is usually handled by the receiving teller. As a rule a pass book will be given to the offender in the regular way, but no money will be paid out by the bank until it ascertains if the check is good, and which, by ordinary methods, usually requires two days' time, and longer if the check be drawn on a far distant bank. On the day following the opening of the account the offender will visit the bank and on this occasion approaches the paying teller. Of course, he is not known to the paying teller, but he produces his pass book and shows the paying teller that he has on deposit say one hundred dollars. He asks to withdraw fifty. Hundreds of paying tellers have been caught off their guard with this game by neglecting to look up the party's account, and in an unguarded moment take it for granted that the party's account is O. K.

Stolen pass books are an extensive source of loss to banks. Throughout the country thousands of foreigners have savings accounts in banks. With most of them it is customary to keep the bank books in their trunks or rooms where they can easily be stolen by one of their countrymen, who takes the book to the bank, impersonates the owner and obtains the cash.

To illustrate the importance that the detective must give to the small details when making an investigation, I was once called upon to investigate a forgery that had been perpetrated upon a bank in a town of about twenty thousand population. In this case a middle aged woman presented a check and obtained eighty dollars thereon, the check later proving to be a forgery. I questioned the paying teller for an hour, but he seemed unable to assist me and could say nothing about the woman except that she was of middle age and pleasant appearing. This, however, was very vague, as there were in the town probably five hundred women who were pleasant appearing and of middle age. I persisted in having the paying teller revert his mind to the occasion of the woman's visit to the bank, and he finally recalled that the woman wore a pin bearing the emblem of a secret society of some kind— he could not recall which. I immediately set to work, and later in the day submitted to the paying teller a dozen or more lodge emblems, when he selected the emblem of the Order of the Eastern Star as being identical with what the woman wore. The foregoing consumed one day, and the next morning I set about ascertaining what member of the Order of the Eastern Star in that town or vicinity would have been likely to pass the forged check. From the secretary of the order I obtained a list of the members, then decided to take the secretary into my confidence and asked him who of the members he thought would have been most likely to commit this crime. His suspicions rested upon a woman who lived in a village just outside of the town, and from all he told me I became convinced she was the woman wanted.

The next morning, accompanied by the paying teller, I called at the woman's home under a pretext, and when the paying teller promptly identified her as being the woman for whom he cashed the check.

Many large sums of money have been obtained through forgery. The most remarkable case ever brought to my attention was one that involved $30,000.00. A man forty years of age had been made the business agent of a wealthy lady who was some eighty years old. This man was also named in the lady's will to be the executor of her estate after her death. It happened, however, that this man died first and among his papers and effects was found a note for $30,000.00 purporting to have been signed by the woman in favor of this man. When claim was made upon her for the amount of this note she promptly denied having ever signed such a note, and pronounced the note a forgery, and so the note was never paid. In this particular case it occurred to me that the man no doubt believed that the woman for whom he was business agent would, in all probability, die first, and when it would have been an easy matter for him, as executor, to have taken possession of the amount of the note. Because of the prominence of all parties concerned in this case, it was never given publicity.

Raised checks are an extensive source of loss and annoyance to banks and individuals. Many checks, after being written, mailed or sent, fall into the hands of persons who make a practice of "raising" the amounts for which the checks were originally intended and written, and then pass or have them cashed. For instance, a check written for ten dollars will be raised to one hundred dollars, or to whatever amount the raiser may believe it can be passed without arousing the suspicions of the bank, merchant or individual upon whom it is to be passed. I have seen many raised checks, the favorite method of the latter day check raiser being to remove from the check with chemicals the figures and wording of the amounts, and then to insert a greater amount. The original signature of the drawer of the check is of course left intact. It often requires the aid of a magnifying glass to discover the erasure or removal of the original writing. When necessary the name of the payee is also removed and another name inserted.

CHAPTER V

CONFESSIONS

As in other criminal cases, when confessions are obtained from forgers, it is a good plan to take the same in writing in the presence of reliable witnesses, and to have the confession signed by the criminal. However, great care must be exercised when taking a statement or confession from a criminal, and even though the statement or confession is given voluntarily and willingly by the criminal, it should be embodied in the statement in writing that the same is so given, that it is given without any threats or coercion having been made or resorted to, and that it is given without promise of reward or compensation. Such a statement should also show that it has been explained to the person before signing it that he or she understands that the same may be used against him or her later.

For the average case I would suggest a statement worded about as follows, or in accordance with the kind of case it is to apply to:

"I, Jone Doe, wish to state that on June 30th, 1914, I entered the First National Bank and obtained $50.00 cash upon a check which I knew to be a forgery, and to which check I signed the name of John Smith, without Mr. Smith's permission or authorization, and which check I represented to the bank as having been signed by John Smith. I was arrested today by Detective John Brown, who has not threatened nor coerced me in any way, neither have I been promised any reward, compensation or leniency for making this statement, and I understand this statement may be used against me."

Having persons make affidavit to statements of this nature does not strengthen them in any way, since the law permits persons to repudiate affidavits without constituting perjury, so long as the affidavit or statement has not been given in any judicial proceeding.

In connection with the investigation of forgery cases I might add that it is a good plan to have the person whose signature was forged make an affidavit that the check or other paper repudiated by him, was not signed by him and not authorized by him. I once had a case of forgery wherein it was neglected to do this. When the offender was arrested he proved to be a close friend of the man whose signature was forged. Then to save his friend from prosecution the man went to the bank and stated that the check which he had at first repudiated was his own signed check.

CHAPTER VI

MURDER CASES

In my experience with murder cases I would divide such crimes into three classes, namely: The cases wherein a murder has been carefully planned or premeditated; the cases where a murder is committed suddenly or on the spur of the moment; and those that are a result of some person intending only to do bodily harm to another but wherein such injuries later cause death. One could hardly lay down any set rule to be applied by the detective for the proper investigation of murder cases. There are, however, several primary things that should be kept in mind by the detective, and which I have found will apply in most murder cases. The first and most important thing to be looked into is the motive. Every effort should be made by the detective to establish the motive, and if successful he will, as a rule, have little difficulty in ascertaining the identity of the murderer. After the murderer's identity is known the detective has something definite upon which to work.

The detective should satisfy himself as to which of the three classes previously named the crime would come under. It should be borne in mind that murders as a rule, are not committed for pastime or amusement. I would venture to state that seventy-five per cent of murders committed come under the first named class. Often they are very carefully planned and the plans just as carefully executed. The detective should ascertain, by making inquiry or otherwise, who would profit by the death of the person murdered. It should be ascertained if robbery was the direct motive.

Hundreds of persons have been murdered by slow poisoning. In such cases the detective must look for the relative who would benefit by the death of the person murdered. Persons very often are murdered so that the insurance they may carry can be claimed. It should be ascertained if the person murdered had any quarrels with business associates, relatives, friends, or other persons, or if the enmity of any person in particular was incurred at any time. If a weapon was used to cause death, it should be ascertained from the nature of the wound what kind of weapon was used, and if the weapon prove to be a pistol, its calibre, make, etc., should be gone into. Regardless of the kind of weapon used, if its nature can be established, the detective should endeavor to learn where it was secured, who was known to be in possession of, or known to have carried such a weapon. In murder cases every clue, no matter how small or vague, should be run out by the detective. The smallest clues often develop the best results. As the circumstances in every murder case will differ, the detective must use his own judgment as to how to proceed. Application of good judgment and good common sense methods have never failed to bring about results.

CHAPTER VII

GRAFTERS

A class of criminals who are, in my opinion, the most obnoxious of any the detective may have to deal with, and of which class only a small percentage are detected and convicted are the grafters. I will venture to state that not more than one such criminal in every hundred finds his way behind prison bars, where all thieves of this class rightly belong. The general public cannot perceive how prevalent this form of stealing has become. The reason probably is because the grafter of today usually moves in the best society and often holds a position of trust, which facts tend to divert suspicion from him and from his crooked dealings.

I am sure that a successful career awaits any ambitious young detective who will devote his time and energy to hunting down grafters. One or two successful cases will start the detective on the road to success. The field for detectives for this class of work is unlimited, remuneration is the best, and better still, the grafter is by far the easiest of all criminals to catch. It is as easy to catch grafters as it is to catch fish, the process being simply a matter of baiting a hook; the grafter, in his greed for money, will do the rest.

In both large and small cities, and in country districts as well, grafters are daily gathering in ill gotten money in many different ways. Criminal records of most of our states show that men, while holding important positions of trust in our state departments, have been detected and found guilty of various forms of grafting. The same records, in a good many of our large cities, will show the same. I believe that one of the best things that could possibly be done by the governors of our states, by the mayors of our cities, and by our prosecuting attorneys, would be to employ annually a first-class, reliable detective to investigate thoroughly into the various interests of the public which they control to ascertain if grafting exists. Grafting has usually been found where such investigations have been made.

The various ways by which men who have held official positions in state, county and city governments have been known to profit by grafting would be a long story to relate. Regarding grafting by public officials, there is one thing in particular that the detective should always keep in mind, that being that political records show that thousands of men throughout the country have had themselves elected to public office, the full term of which netted them in salary often only half the amount expended by them in having themselves elected to office. When such persons are elected to public office it very often is the beginning of grafting by them in some form.

We will grant that some of these men were public spirited citizens, and while in office may have served the public at their own expense. Nevertheless, when we know that a man has actually bought his way, and paid dearly to have himself elected to office, that man will at least bear watching. I have in mind the case of a certain county official in a western state, who, some years ago, succeeded in having himself elected to office, which office, for its entire term of three years, carried a salary amounting to $2,400.00. This man was known to have expended close to $5,000.00 to become elected. Within a year after taking office he was ousted by the people of the county, who demanded his resignation, it having been found that his campaign for election was financed by a certain manufacturing company, and that after taking office he had accepted certain additional sums of money to protect the interests of the same concern.

Right here we have another kind of grafter. The man just mentioned was known to have purchased outright with money, at so much per vote, hundreds of votes that were cast for his election. Voters accepting such money are of course guilty of a crime worse than grafting. In most of our states we now have laws which make it a misdemeanor for anyone to pay or promise to pay, or to give or promise to give anything for any person's vote.

Grafting of the worst kind has been found to exist in the law making bodies of some of our states. Many state legislators have been convicted through having accepted money to vote for or against certain measures, when by so doing they virtually sold out, for considerations of money, the people by whom they were elected to faithfully represent. The methods employed by most grafters, I believe, are too common and too well known to need mention.

In connection with grafting in county and city governments, it has been found very often that officials whose duties were to protect society, and to endeavor to stamp out and to prevent certain violations of the law, were grafters of the worst type. For considerations of money they guaranteed protection to persons known to be violating the law. Such protection has been guaranteed in many of our large cities by police officials to keepers of houses of ill repute, to keepers of gambling dens, or blind tigers, etc. The extent to which such grafting is done can easily be ascertained by the detective if he will cultivate the acquaintance of the keepers of such places. And now a few words as to how the detective may set about catching some of these various kinds of grafters.

One good way for the detective to secure evidence against a grafter is to first form his acquaintance, then lead him to believe, and make it plain to him that he also is a grafter, or at least willing to be one. After such confidence is established, an arrangement should be made for making any payments of money to the grafter at such a place and in such a manner that it can be substantially corroborated. So as to make this point more clear, I will illustrate how I once, as a result of one day's work, secured confessions from some forty grafters in connection with vote buying in one county just previous to an election.

It was suspected that a certain candidate for office was spending large sums of money for votes and I was called in to obtain positive proof of it. After being supplied with a list of names of persons believed to be the distributors of the candidate's money, I purposely selected from the list a man said to be the smartest of the lot. A few hours later, accompanied by an assistant, I called upon the man at his home. I advised him that while we were strangers to him we were old friends of the candidate's and that we had been called upon to assist in his campaign.

After discussing local conditions with the man, and the prospect of our friend's election to office, I took from my pocket two hundred dollars in bills which had previously been marked, and handed them to the man saying that our friend the candidate sent the money to give to him for distribution. Needless to state, the man did not refuse to take the money. The bold and confident manner in which it was handed to him laid at rest any fears or suspicions he may have had. He no doubt felt satisfied that we were grafters of his own type, and immediately began to talk very freely with us. We conversed with him for probably an hour, during which time he advised us of various sums of money given him by the candidate for distribution, also gave us the names of a dozen or more men who were distributing funds for the candidate.

Before the day was over we had this man arrested and searched, when all of the marked money was found on his person. Realizing that he had been trapped, he lost no time making a confession, in which he implicated others, with the result that some forty confessions were secured. I have found grafters of this kind very prevalent practically all over the country, and, as a rule, a good detective will experience little trouble finding some honest, public-spirited citizen willing to defray the cost of detective hire to run down such persons.

Regarding another kind of grafter, I once was called upon to secure evidence in a certain small town against a county official who was believed to be guaranteeing protection to persons selling liquor in violation of the law, the chief violators being several local druggists. Shortly after arriving in the town I began to negotiate in a business like way for the purchase of one of the drug stores. I found the proprietor of one of the stores willing to sell out provided he secured his price. After remaining in town about ten days, I took an option for thirty days on one of the stores, for which option I paid a hundred dollars. I then left town temporarily, telling the druggist I was returning to my home town to consult with my partner in business.

Within a week I returned with my partner (another detective) and who expressed himself as being satisfied with the place I had negotiated for. We told the druggist we were ready to buy, but before closing the deal had decided we would like to be assured against interference by the authorities in case we saw fit to sell liquor in our store. I suppose because he believed he was getting his own price for his property and business, the druggist responded quite easily. As we expected he would do, he volunteered to take us and introduce us to the very county official we were after, and which he did that evening.

The druggist explained to the county official that we were to purchase his property and business the next day, and that we were naturally anxious to know if we could be assured of protection in case we decided to sell liquor. Everything appearing to be regular to the official, he told us very bluntly what it would cost us per year to be protected and requested a first payment of $50.00. I advised him we did not have so much cash with us, and finally arranged that he call upon us the next day at 10 a. m. at my room at the local hotel, when we would make the payment.

Early the next morning at the hotel we secreted two responsible persons in a closet in my room, then awaited the arrival of our grafter. He came at the appointed hour and we again discussed the matter of our protection and paid him $50.00. Immediately afterwards our witnesses stepped out of the closet, and finding himself caught with four witnesses against him, the man readily agreed to give us a written and signed confession. He was told he would have to resign his position forthwith or be prosecuted. He chose the former, which ended the case.

The dictagraph has played an important part in the detection and conviction of grafters. When it is suspected that state, county or city officials are grafting, in order to detect them, we will take for example one or more city officials whose duty it is to let for their city, contracts for paving. When a municipality gets ready to pave three or four streets, or to let contracts for machinery, buildings or other public improvements, specifications are drawn and the same advertised. Perhaps twenty contractors will submit bids and one can imagine the rivalry that may exist among the contractors, especially since the municipality usually reserves the right to reject any or all bids and are not bound to let any given contract to the lowest bidder. Then naturally and very often the question arises as to who shall be favored. My experience in many cases has been that when the city officials are open to taking graft, a contract will go to the contractor who will pay the most for being favored.

Three city officials once were trapped when a detective spent six months in their city posing as a contractor, and finally when his company was favored with a street paving contract upon the payment of $500.00 cash, he arranged to talk over the transaction and later paid over the money in a room in a hotel in which a dictagraph was secretly installed, and which made it possible to substantiate the transaction from start to finish.

Grafting is prevalent in many lines of business, especially where one man is entrusted with the letting of contracts, or with the purchase of supplies for a city, corporation, factory or individual. The following will illustrate just how prevalent petty grafting has become and which came to my notice through a case I had occasion to investigate for a certain well-to-do gentleman. This man owned two automobiles and entrusted to his colored chauffeur the purchase of gasoline and supplies for the machines. From various dealers this chauffeur obtained a "rake-off" on every gallon of gasoline used, and on the purchase of new tires, etc. The more gasoline he used the more money this chauffeur would make, and the same with tires and other supplies. During the investigation this chauffeur's purchases of gasoline from the dealer were compared with the mileage of the automobiles, and when it was estimated that the owner was paying for two or three gallons of gasoline per week for a long time that could not possibly have been used. It was then believed that the chauffeur was selling the surplus gasoline, but this could not be proven. Finally, when taken to task and shown the amount of his purchases, he confessed to having poured the gasoline into the sewer of the garage.

I was once called upon to look into a case where grafting was suspected in a small town, and where the president of the town council, who was a prominent physician, was under suspicion. I arrived in town two days before a certain measure was to be acted upon in council, the measure being in relation to a heating contract. I called upon the physician at his office and told him in plain words that I represented one of the competing firms and that I had been authorized to offer him two hundred dollars for his vote and influence in favor of my company. He accepted from me the two hundred dollars cash consisting of marked five dollar bills, and endeavored to convince me that he was not a grafter by saying that he had intended favoring my company anyway and was not accepting the money for changing his decision on the measure in council.

After leaving him I went promptly to the persons who had retained me, when it was quickly arranged to have a certain person who owed the physician a small bill go there to pay it with a twenty dollar bill. This party returned with three of the marked five dollar bills, which the physician unsuspectingly made the change with. In addition, I had had the physician prescribe for me for a pretended ailment, and by which I was enabled to substantiate my call upon him, in spite of the fact that I went to him alone. It was only desired to have this man resign from council, which, it may be imagined, he was glad to do when confronted with the evidence of having accepted a bribe. This entire case was closed successfully in less than four hours after active work was started.

CHAPTER VIII

DETECTIVE WORK IN DEPARTMENT STORES

There are, in my opinion, no business concerns that suffer a greater loss, nor are occasioned more worry than are the department stores of our large cities. Annually they lose thousands of dollars worth of merchandise mainly through the operations of store thieves known as shoplifters, and through the dishonesty of employes. In any of our large up-to-date department stores the services of no less than a dozen trained detectives, both male and female, are required to properly guard such stores against thefts. Inasmuch as department stores offer one of the broadest fields for private detectives, I shall set forth some of the many ways by which such stores are robbed and defrauded daily; also one of the best known methods for detectives to cope with the offenders.

As previously stated, in department stores, both male and female detectives are employed. Although I have known instances where experienced female store detectives have been of valuable assistance to department stores, male detectives, as a rule, can give the best protection. The store detective must be a person of good, sound judgment, be able to think and act quickly, and must always be alert and wide awake during business hours at the store where he or she may be engaged. It is essential that store detectives dress well, but not conspicuously, and while in the store, if the detective be a man, he should wear his hat and coat at all times.

If it be in the winter time the detective should wear a light overcoat, and on rainy days should carry an umbrella. It is a very good plan for the detective to carry a package under his arm, the purpose of all these things being to give out the impression that the detective is a customer instead of what he really is. The detective should keep moving about in the store, pretend to make purchases, and if possible change his hat and coat several times a day.

In order to emphasize the necessity of these things, we will look at shoplifting for a few moments from the shoplifter's point of view. Usually when a shoplifter decides upon some particular store to operate in, he or she may first visit the store a dozen times if necessary in order to pick out the store detective. After becoming satisfied on this point the shoplifter figures on how best to avoid the persons he or she have picked out as being detectives, then will begin to operate.

The professional shoplifter, if she be a woman, usually wears, during cold weather, a long coat and wide skirt in which are capacious pockets for concealing and carrying off stolen merchandise. The shoplifter rarely will bother with cheap merchandise, but will confine her thefts to valuable laces, silks, furs, jewelry, etc., which she secretes in the pockets of her skirt or coat. During the summer season when it would be out of place to wear a coat, the shoplifter takes advantage of the rainy days and enters stores with her umbrella, in which she secretes and carries off such articles as she may find an opportunity to take from the counters unobserved by the clerks or floorwalkers.

Very often a professional shoplifter will take with her to a store a confederate, especially if she has reason to believe that her operations have aroused the suspicions of any of the store's detectives. The confederate will proceed directly to the ladies' toilet or rest room. After the shoplifter has taken one or more articles she joins her confederate, and unobserved passes the articles to the confederate. Then in case she has been watched or is arrested upon leaving the store, no goods will be found on her person.

I have known careless store detectives to arrest shoplifters whom they observed stealing goods in the store, but who did not have the goods on their persons when they were arrested. When an arrest of this kind is made it is usually the beginning of serious trouble for the management of the store. The detective will have played into the hands of the shoplifter; she will promptly take advantage of the circumstances and bring suit against the management for false arrest. Ordinarily department stores do not relish such undesirable notoriety; damage suits are expensive, so usually they settle such cases. If the shoplifter, after having been observed taking some article, enters the rest or toilet room before leaving the store, it will be best for the detective not to take any chances in causing her arrest for the reason just mentioned.

The detective, as a rule, should not make an arrest under any circumstances until after the shoplifter has left the store. I have known cases where shoplifters and store thieves were arrested inside of stores with stolen goods on their persons, but who, immediately after being arrested, set up the claim that they had no intention of stealing the goods, but that they were just taking the goods to the light to examine them. Later when their cases came up in court they would be represented by shrewd attorneys who took advantage of the law itself by maintaining that inasmuch as the goods had not been taken from the premises of the store, no theft was committed.

I would state that as a rule if the detective is watchful he will have no difficulty in picking out the shoplifters. Persons so bent usually keep looking about them furtively to note if anyone is watching them. Quite often they are nervous and flit quickly from one counter to another. If the detective be in doubt he usually can, with half an hour's careful watching, determine to his own satisfaction the real purpose of any person's visit to the store.

Department stores suffer serious losses through the operations of other classes of criminals who make a practice of preying on such stores. A large department store of the present day may have on its list from one to two thousand customers, who have with the store what are known as charge accounts. Such customers may visit the store, make a purchase, and have the amount of same charged to their account. Often they make such purchases by telephone, or may send a maid or other person to the store to make the purchases. A certain class of store swindlers make it a point to ascertain the names of persons having such accounts at stores after which they visit the stores, impersonate the customers, and very frequently secure and make off with goods of great value.

Usually such swindlers are not discovered until the end of a month, when the customer receives his or her bill, but by which time the swindler may be in some distant city preparing to victimize another store. Dishonest employes and discharged employes are usually responsible for giving out information regarding customers' charge accounts. The swindler, however, can easily secure such information in many other ways. We have also the store swindler who goes to some large city and purposely registers at a leading hotel. He then visits a department store, purchases an expensive suit or overcoat, in payment of which he tenders a bogus check. He requests that his purchase be delivered to his hotel, which may be done, but the swindler will be gone long before the store discovers that it can not realize on the check.

One may ask how stores can be so easily victimized. There are two reasons, and they apply not only to this class of swindle, but to many others as well. The swindler may have, by his smooth and suave manner, impressed the management or clerk that he was all that he represented himself to be, and they, in an unguarded moment, allowed themselves to be swindled. On the other hand, it may have been the anxiety of making a sale at a good profit with an apparently good customer that may have caused them to overlook ascertaining the genuineness of the swindler's check before delivering the goods.

Another source of loss by department stores is through dishonest clerks being in collusion with outside parties. A clerk, for instance, employed at a silk or lace counter, will have a friend or confederate call at her counter during the day. A yard of silk may be purchased and paid therefor, but it is quite an easy matter for the dishonest clerk to cut off and have wrapped a yard and a half or two yards of the material purchased. I have known respectable, well-to-do women enter into such arrangements with clerks at stores, seemingly treating such matters lightly, and even telling their friends about such transactions.

There are innumerable other ways by which employes steal from stores. Some clerks inclined to steal become very bold and very often carry out openly stolen goods that they claim to have purchased. At thoroughly up-to-date stores all clerks and employes, when leaving the store in the evening, are required to leave by some certain exit, where there is stationed a watchman who examines all packages that are carried out. The watchman holds up all packages that do not bear the O. K. of some floorwalker or other official of the store.

During such times as the Christmas shopping season, which in large cities begins about November first, the management of large stores find it necessary to double their detective forces, and well they may, as November and December are the months during which shoplifters, pickpockets and others figure on reaping their harvests. Pickpockets in stores must also be given attention by the store detective. Customers do not relish having their purses or pockets picked while in stores, and when it does happen to a customer, he or she usually remains away from that store in the future. Much more might be said upon the subject of department store detective work, but I believe what has been gone into will be sufficient to guide the average person in this branch of the work.

CHAPTER IX

RAILROAD DETECTIVE WORK

Railroad companies suffer tremendous losses yearly in spite of the fact that vast sums are continually being spent to guard against theft by employees, thefts by car thieves, damage suits, etc. As to the first mentioned source of loss railroad companies are obliged to maintain at their freight yards and terminals large forces of detectives to guard against thefts. Although not generally known to persons outside of railroad circles, it is a fact that many roads employ an average of fifty detectives for every hundred miles of their systems. The large railroads nowadays are policed in much the same manner as are our large cities.

Besides guarding against thefts of valuable freight while in transit, patrons at the crowded stations and depots must be protected so far as possible from the operations of pickpockets, swindlers and baggage thieves. The smaller stations along the line where there are ticket offices must be guarded against attacks by burglars. Practically all large railroads maintain staffs of detectives whose duties are to travel over the lines and do what is called checking. Manipulation of tickets and cash fares is usually prevalent and no doubt will always be so long as we have railroads and conductors.

Trains are checked at regular intervals unknown to train crews. Action of train crews while on duty are reported on by detectives; also the kind of service accorded patrons of dining, parlor and sleeping cars. In these days when competition is keen, and when railroads are vying with each other to furnish the best possible service, it is important to managements to know to a certainty if conductors and other employees are courteous and obliging to patrons, if any rules of the company are being disregarded, and, as a whole, if the kind of service that it is intended to give is being given.

Checking passenger trains is one of the most congenial branches of detective work, and a branch which gives the young detective plenty of valuable experience. This branch of railroad detective work being the most desirable, I will endeavor to show what managements usually expect from their detectives. The detective may be detailed to check a sleeping car on some particular line from the time of departure of the car from some given point in the evening until it arrives at its destination in the morning. The detective's report will be expected to contain information about as follows:

Name of the conductor in charge of the car; if the crew got out at stations to assist passengers to board or alight; if the stepping box was properly placed for passengers; if assistance was given with baggage; if the conductor and porter were wearing their proper uniforms; if uniforms were neat, and if the conductor and porter were courteous to passengers. If the car was properly cleaned and dusted; if the porter unnecessarily disturbed the passengers in any way; if all berths were made up properly, and if properly closed in the morning; if the window shades worked properly; if hammocks were properly hung in berths; if the linen was clean and the lights in good order; if the lights were turned out at the proper hour; if any persons at stations disturbed passengers; if any of the crew loafed in any unoccupied berths. If there were any complaints by passengers and if the complaints were attended to. If ventilation was good and proper temperatures maintained; if any of the crew slept while on duty; if the water and towel supply was proper and sufficient; if there were any accidents during the trip; if porter had shoes properly polished.

If passengers were properly brushed by the porter; if any of the crew acted familiarly with passengers; if any of the crew smoked while on duty; if tickets were collected promptly by the conductor, and if railway and hotel guides were in proper places. In addition to the foregoing the detective usually is required to report on how many berths were occupied in the car, the number of men and number of women passengers, children if any, also how many cash fares were collected by the conductor for berths. When reporting on dining car service detectives usually are expected to cover in their reports the following:

If crew was polite and efficient; if conductor was properly uniformed, amount of the detective's check and its number; if linen was in good condition and clean; if tables were properly set; if food was of good quality. If waiters were properly uniformed; if finger bowls were promptly and correctly served; if dining car was properly ventilated and lighted; if liquor was served on the car; if silver was in good condition and prompt service given. The articles of food and drink ordered by the detective should be shown, the number of the table at which he sat, the number of the waiter who served him, the number of the car, the time he left the car, the number of the train, its time of departure and arrival, and between what points traveled.

With such daily reports placed in their hands, persons responsible to the managements for proper maintenance of sleeping and dining car service are enabled to know precisely the kind of service that is being given patrons, which information enables them to keep such service to the highest standard of efficiency. Employees often, when coming in from a run, are summarily discharged, or their resignations may be asked for, but that is another matter; railroads need and must have detectives. It will be seen that the railroads offer a very broad field for detectives, and there is no reason why any young man with good common sense should not be able to properly check a sleeping or dining car on his first attempt.

CHAPTER X

DETECTIVE WORK FOR STREET RAILWAYS

Practically all street railway companies find it necessary to employ detectives. The largest corporations of this kind may employ anywhere from ten to fifty detectives the year round, and one may wonder why and how all these detectives are employed. Street railway companies, like the railroad companies, are obliged continually to guard against three serious sources of loss, namely: thefts by employees, damage suits and strikes. Experience has taught the management of street railway companies that stealing on the part of conductors is always more or less prevalent. Conductors are not usually prosecuted when caught stealing fares, but are simply discharged. The morning and evening crowds on street cars provide opportunities for conductors to steal, if they may be so inclined.

A conductor may feel that half a dozen fares appropriated to his own use every day will not be missed by the company. However, if we take a corporation employing say five or six hundred conductors, it will readily be seen that small thefts by conductors can easily run into hundreds of dollars daily. As a rule managements do not discharge a conductor for stealing until it has been found conclusively, on at least two or three occasions, that he is doing so. Usually there are as many detectives employed on street railway lines as there are runs or routes on the system. Unknown to the conductors these detectives ride on the cars from early morning until evening, or from morning until midnight, changing from one line to another frequently enough not to be noticed by the conductors.

The detective provides himself with a small counting machine which can be concealed in the hand. Upon boarding a car he makes note of the number of the car, the cap number of the conductor, and the number of cash fares shown by the register. While apparently busily engaged reading a newspaper or magazine, the detective keeps accurate count of the number of passengers boarding the car, noting at the same time if transfers are received or issued. As a rule conductors are required to render separate reports to the company for every trip they make, and to show the place and minute the trip was terminated. They must show in their reports the number of cash fares collected; also the number of transfers issued and collected.

If a conductor's report for any given trip does not coincide with the report of the detective the conductor will be checked more closely on succeeding trips, often by as many as three detectives at the same time. If the conductor's reports to the company continue to show a shortage of cash fares, the chances are that he will be discharged. As to the second mentioned source of loss, managements of large companies usually are obliged to defend in the courts the year round, damage suits brought against them for personal injuries by persons who very frequently have sustained no injury or damage whatever. A surprisingly large number of fake suits are entered yearly against transportation companies. There is also to deal with the professional witnesses, who go from place to place, and who, for considerations of money, will swear to having seen anything happen.

I recall a case wherein a middle aged lady left her home one morning in New York to board a steamship bound for Europe. She rode down town in a surface car which happened to collide with another car, with the result that half a dozen passengers were more or less injured. The lady in question, however, sustained no injury and continued on her way. Several months later, while at the home of a relative in England, she accidentally fell and injured her spine. She promptly took advantage of her mishap by returning to New York, where she brought suit against the railway corporation, claiming to have been disabled permanently as a result of the street car accident before sailing for Europe. The fact that she was permanently injured could not be disputed; the railway was not prepared to dispute the matter of where and how she claimed to have received her injuries, with the result that she received heavy damages. The fraud was discovered by chance several years later.

Like all other large employers of labor, street railway companies are not immune from having their employes go out on strike. When street railway employees, or those of other transportation companies are organized, a strike is liable to be called at any time, and often upon the least provocation. It is highly important that managements have advance information of any proposed strike, and of any grievances of any employees, whether well founded or not. By having such advance information serious loss can very often be averted by the management getting rid of the agitators and trouble makers as quickly as they make their appearance among the employes. It is well for the managements to keep advised at all times regarding the attitude of employees.

There is but one good way to accomplish this, and that is to have detectives scattered among the employes. The detectives can be put to work among the men as conductors, motormen or as shop men. I have known detectives to work in each of these capacities for years at a stretch without becoming uncovered, and without their purpose having become known. The valuable services that such detectives can render their employers will readily be appreciated.

CHAPTER XI

OTHER KINDS OF DETECTIVE WORK

I believe it will be of interest to both experienced and inexperienced detectives to be enlightened regarding some of the many other sources from which private detective work arises. Lawyers throughout the country, in both large and small cities, and even in thinly settled country communities, are large employers of private detective service. When prosecuting or defending damage cases, attorneys very often need detective service in getting at facts, in order to properly prepare their cases. Witnesses must be interviewed, and very often investigated. Murder, burglary, damage and divorce cases supply needs for a great deal of detective work.

State, county and city governments are large employers of private detectives. Counties and cities often have their own staffs of detectives, but there are many occasions when special detectives must be pressed into service. Nowadays election frauds are practiced practically everywhere. Private detectives are needed and can easily obtain employment wherever there are professional politicians. Trusted employees often go wrong and disappear with public funds. Officials holding high offices very often turn out to be embezzlers. Dozens of banks are being defrauded daily somewhere by forgers, sneak thieves and others. Hundreds of our large banking institutions periodically place under surveillance their entire staffs of employees, from the cashier down to the messenger boy and porter in order to keep advised regarding the habits and associates of the employees, which information enables them to select from time to time the proper persons for promotion.

Large manufacturers, no matter what the line, usually are extensive employers of private detectives. I have in mind a large manufacturing concern which employs in its factory probably three thousand persons, and at all times not less than two hundred traveling salesmen, also dozens of branch managers. When it is suspected that a traveling salesman is not attending to business, he is placed under surveillance while on his travels from city to city, for probably one, two or three weeks. The detective's report will show the time of day the salesman begins work, what firms he calls on, how much time spent with each firm, and how much time is idled away, and the time the salesman discontinued work each day; also how much time the salesman may spend in saloons or other places, how he spends his evenings and how much money he spends.

In connection with this class of detective work, I once had occasion to keep under surveillance for three weeks a traveling salesman, who, as it developed, devoted more time to a side line than he did to the line he was being paid to travel and promote business for. Needless to state, this salesman, after his employers received my reports, was obliged to change his ways. The tendency of salesmen to devote time to side lines is one of the worst evils that employers of traveling salesmen have to contend with.

In factories, no matter of what nature, employers usually find it expedient to place secretly among their employees, detectives who work side by side with the employees. Male or female detectives are so placed, as the case may warrant. The reports these detectives are enabled to render show which employees are worthy of trust or promotion and those that are not. Such reports will show who are the lazy ones, the dissatisfied ones, the strike agitators, those who steal tools, material or supplies, those who violate any rules of the factory or shop; also what kind of treatment is accorded the employees by the foreman. An entire book could be written on this branch of detective work alone. It is an undisputed fact that large employers of labor nowadays cannot conduct their business as successfully without secret service work.

Besides the thousands of manufactories, transportation companies and others who constantly employ detectives, we have the wholesale companies who deal in groceries, dry goods, drugs, shoes, etc., who also are in need of such services. The traveling salesman of such concerns must be looked after, also the drones and thieves with which their warehouses become infested.

ILLEGAL LIQUOR SELLING

Illegal liquor selling opens a very broad field for detectives throughout the country, and I have personally obtained and directed the obtaining of evidence in a hundred different ways. In this branch of the work one cannot be guided by any set rule, but must be governed by prevailing conditions. If it be desired to obtain evidence regarding the illegal sale of liquor, or regarding any other violations of law in a hotel of any size, there is only one good plan, and that is to have the detective obtain employment at the place for a few weeks or a month.

I have had many occasions to direct the work of obtaining evidence of the illegal sale of liquor, gambling and other vices in small towns. In the average town of from three to ten thousand population, the best plan is to have the detective obtain employment in some mill, factory or store. In this way he can easily become acquainted and can associate with whatever element he may choose to associate with and without his purpose being suspected. After the detective has been in the town for two or three weeks, and has purchased liquor at the various places where it is sold illegally, a second detective is sent to the town who poses as the friend of the first one. The first detective then proceeds to take his friend around to the various places in the evening, or on Sunday, and in this way corroborative evidence is obtained. Bottles of liquor should be obtained at the various places and retained intact for use later as evidence.

ANONYMOUS LETTERS

There are written and mailed every year thousands of anonymous letters, threatening and otherwise, and there is need for much detective work along this line. Many such letters are written and addressed with the typewriter, the authors believing that by so writing them they can escape detection. But this is not so, as I have always found it easier to trace to the writer those that are written with typewriter, because when type is placed under the magnifying glass it is found that type differs considerably on every typewriter, and each set of type has its own peculiarities. With the assistance of an able typewriter expert, I was enabled during the course of one year to clear up three anonymous letter cases wherein the letters were written with a typewriter.

Thousands of letters known as "black hand" letters are mailed and sent throughout the country, the sending of which offers a wide field for investigation. "Black Hand" letters are by no means all sent by Italians, as is commonly believed. The term is usually applied to letters in which sums of money are anonymously demanded, upon threats of death, torture or punishment.

"ROPING"

The term "roping" is used in connection with detective work to express cultivating the acquaintance of a criminal or other person for the purpose of learning what the person may know regarding a crime or other matter about which it may be desired to obtain information. There is a vast lot of detective work of this kind done, and I will submit a few cases, since every detective should be proficient along this line.

A man was in charge of the supply department for a large corporation, and was suspected of carrying to his home such articles as light globes, machinists' tools, paint, stamped envelopes, soap, towels, etc. Being called upon to verify this, I detailed a female detective on the case, who succeeded in obtaining lodging and board at the house, and in two weeks she had seen and brought away more than fifty different kinds of articles that had been stolen and carried home by this man.

I once directed the investigation of an $8,000.00 jewel theft which was brought to a successful close by having a negro detective "rope" a negro waiter. The jewels in question were inadvertently left lying on a chair in a cafe by a well known actress, and they were not missed until the following morning. Three negro waiters came under suspicion and finally suspicion was narrowed down to one of them, who, after the theft, kept roving from city to city. Although he was kept under close surveillance for a period of four months he was never seen with any of the stolen jewels, and apparently made no effort to dispose of them. The suspect finally obtained a position as waiter in a fashionable cafe in a certain large city, when I arranged for a similar position at the same cafe for a negro detective, who immediately began cultivating the acquaintance of the suspect. After two weeks he told the suspect that he was worried over the fear of arrest for having stolen some jewelry in another city. This caused the suspect to feel safe in confiding to the detective the fact that he also had stolen some jewels and was worried over the matter. On a certain night they arranged to meet at the suspect's room to show each other their stolen jewels, the detective arranging for this so as to ascertain where the suspect was keeping his. The suspect was arrested the following day, and at his room practically all of the stolen jewels were recovered.

I have handled a great many cases wherein the acquaintance of persons holding confidential positions were cultivated. For example, men who employ private secretaries often desire to know if the secretary is absolutely reliable and trustworthy. Whether the secretary be man or woman, "roping" is resorted to, to ascertain if such persons would divulge secrets of their employers. "Roping" of this class of people often entails great expense and detective work of a very high order. I have handled several cases wherein it was necessary to have the detective, in order to get acquainted in a natural way, join the same church and clubs to which the party to be "roped" belonged, also furnished the detective with an automobile and other things so as to keep up appearances, and apparently be on an equal footing with the person to be "roped."

Roping is very frequently resorted to in damage cases, also in theft cases. Many fake damage suits are brought annually against street railway and other transportation companies. While such suits are pending it is a good plan to have a male or female detective, as circumstances may require, get acquainted with, or obtain room and board with the person to be "roped," and which usually results in the detective learning the extent of the person's injuries, if there be any, and such other information of value to attorneys defending such a case.

DETECTIVE WORK IN WAREHOUSES

As previously stated herein, every owner of a wholesale house or warehouse can employ detective service with profit, also packing houses and similar concerns. I have in mind a certain wholesale drug house which employs approximately one hundred men the year round. At one time it was estimated that between two and three hundred dollars worth of goods were stolen and carried off per month. I detailed a detective to go to work in the building among the other employees, and at the end of four weeks the detective's reports showed specific instances of stealing on the part of sixteen employees. The detective was then permitted to discontinue, and I took these sixteen men in hand, one after another, and obtained signed confessions from them relative to their stealings, and all were discharged. I recall that one of these men admitted stealing and carrying off seven Gillette safety razors in a period of two weeks. Also one of the men whom we took in charge, as he was about to quit work for the day, had secreted on his person six different stolen articles.

In the case of a large packing house it was found that drivers were short some of their goods upon arriving at depots, claiming that the missing goods either were stolen or had not been loaded upon their trucks. They made these trips to the depots between midnight and 5 a. m. These drivers with their trucks were shadowed, when it was found that each had along his route a place where goods were unloaded and sold by the driver. In the case of another large packing house I uncovered thefts of butter alone amounting to three hundred pounds per month.

EXPRESS COMPANIES

Express companies are large employers of detective service, because the temptation to steal goods while in transit is very strong with a great many employees. By detailing secret detectives to work with employees, both in the depots and on trains, I have uncovered many thefts. I once obtained a confession from an express messenger who admitted having stolen in one day two dressed turkeys, a loin of pork, two pounds of butter and a quart of whiskey. He admitted these thefts after he was shown that his helper in the express car was a secret detective, who saw him appropriate the articles.

I once had occasion to conduct an investigation for an express company regarding the theft of $1,500.00 worth of unset diamonds, which were stolen while in transit. In the course of three weeks the thief had not been detected, and the nearest that responsibility could be fixed was that the theft was committed by one of three persons. A ruse was then resorted to which produced results, and which ruse often brings results in cases of theft by employees. We caused it to be published in the newspapers that after several weeks investigation and surveillance we had learned the identity of the thief, and that an arrest would positively be made the following day. This had the effect of causing the thief to believe that he had actually been detected, for the next day the stolen diamonds were delivered to the company by mail. The same ruse, applied in various forms, has also been the means of obtaining many confessions in criminal cases. Fear of arrest and conviction often leads a first offender to give up his plunder, and the successful use of this ruse is a matter of bringing it to the attention of the one under suspicion in the most forceful way.

On behalf of an express company, I once was called upon to investigate what was reported to be a burglary of the express office in a town of about five thousand population. Upon arrival there the next day I found that the front window of the office was broken, the break being sufficiently large to have admitted a man's body. I talked with the agent whose breath indicated to me that he had been intoxicated the night previous, and which fact he admitted. This agent had reported to his superiors that upon arrival at the office that morning he found the front window broken, that the safe apparently had not been tampered with, as the key was found to work perfectly. Upon opening the safe he found that two hundred dollars was missing, fifty dollars having been left in the safe by the burglar, according to his statement. Nothing else around the office was stolen or tampered with. In less than five minutes after arriving there I concluded that if any cash had been stolen the agent himself was the guilty one. From a boy outside I learned that the window became broken during a severe electrical storm the previous night, which placed the town in darkness for several hours around midnight. An overhead sign was blown down and crashed through the window. Being further convinced that the agent was guilty and had taken advantage of these circumstances to report a burglary, I asked the agent if he had ever loaned his safe key to anyone, and he replied in the negative. I then told him that I knew how the window had become broken, and asked him if he believed it logical that a thief would take the trouble and risk arrest by having a suitable key made for the safe, enter the building, steal two hundred dollars of the cash and leave fifty there. I told him that in my judgment such would be the work of an employee but not of a burglar. The agent hung his head and I told him I was justified in having him arrested on the spot. He confessed immediately, less than an hour after my arrival upon the scene. The facts as shown in this incident should prove of much worth to the experienced or inexperienced detective.

CONSPIRACIES

The disclosure of conspiracies in their hundreds of forms offers a broad field for the detective. Hundreds of damage suits are instituted annually throughout the country wherein damages claimed to have been suffered by the plaintiff are nothing more than conspiracies to defraud. The field for such investigation is very wide, especially as it applies to fake bankruptcy cases and damage cases brought by persons against railroad and street railway companies. For example, I once investigated a case wherein the store of a certain jewelry firm was destroyed by fire. Later they claimed that during the excitement of the fire some $20,000.00 worth of diamonds were stolen from the premises by some person unknown. The creditors were loath to believe this and had an investigation made which developed that the diamonds in question had not been stolen, but were removed from the store by the owners previous to the fire, and that the fire itself no doubt was a part of the plan to defraud creditors.

Railroad companies suffer tremendously as a result of conspiracies, of which the following is an example, and which case I personally directed: A new railroad was constructed through a certain farming district, for a distance of perhaps fifteen miles. Before the advent of the railroad none of this farming land had ever been valued at more than twenty-five dollars per acre. Practically all the farmers along the line of the railroad claimed damages up to a hundred dollars per acre. The cases were decided in the courts, upon the opinions of viewers who were appointed by the court, and which body of viewers was composed of disinterested farmers of the same county.

After the railroad company had been compelled to pay two or three excessive claims, it looked about for relief, it having suspected right along that a conspiracy existed among the farmers and viewers to claim and recommend such excessive damages. After three cases had been decided against the railroad company, I detailed two detectives to visit these farmers, and who pretended to have been sent by a number of farmers of a far distant county, who also proposed bringing damage suits against a new railroad company; that they had heard of the success these farmers were having with their suits, and that it was desired to know along just what lines they were proceeding. The two detectives also advised the ring leaders that they did not want the information gratis, and if given assistance were authorized to pay a certain percentage of all damages secured in the distant county. The result was these farmers then unsuspectingly told the detectives how they had all met and agreed to claim certain amounts of damages, and how they had even gone so far as to hold mock trials at several of the farmers' homes, so that all concerned would be properly coached when the time came to go into court. At these mock trials one farmer would pose as plaintiff, while another would pose as the railroad company's attorney, when questions were asked, and answers agreed upon, as was anticipated would come out at the real trials or hearings. Needless to state, that after corroborative evidence of this conspiracy was placed in the hands of the railroad company's attorney, no more excessive damages were paid, and I later had the pleasure of being advised that this bit of detective work saved the railroad company fully forty thousand dollars.

As to how creditors are defrauded in hundreds of instances, the following is a fair example: A retail shoe dealer in a middle western state went into bankruptcy owing several eastern jobbers several thousand dollars. Examination of the dealers' stock and records of sales for several months developed the fact that two or three thousand dollars worth of shoes purchased from the eastern jobbers evidently had never entered the dealer's place of business. It was suspected that the merchandise was concealed or had been secretly disposed of by the dealer. I directed an investigation which resulted in locating the goods in another city, the investigation having been conducted along the following lines:

Information as to the road over which the goods were shipped, together with dates, weights and car numbers was first obtained from the shippers. The drayage company on the dealer's end was then seen, after which drivers for the drayage company were interviewed, and which developed information that the missing goods had never been delivered to the dealer's place of business, but instead were moved from one depot to another and promptly re-shipped to another city. The same plan was then followed in that city with the drayage companies and the goods easily located, and which were promptly attached by the creditors.

In another case an Italian fruit jobber once received three carloads of fruit, and after disposing of same left suddenly for parts unknown, without remitting to, or paying the shippers. I was called into this case, and I promptly directed that the Italian's wife and children be placed under close surveillance. In about a week the wife and children packed up their household goods and had the same shipped to a city some three hundred miles distant. The household goods were then watched closely after being unloaded in the freight depot at the point of destination. Three days later the goods were removed from the depot and taken to the home of an Italian, whose house was then kept under surveillance, but no trace could be seen of the fugitive. At the end of a week the household goods were again taken out, hauled to a depot and re-shipped to a small town a hundred miles away. I recall having personally examined the shipping tags attached to the goods upon this occasion, which gave us the address of the final destination of the household goods, and which address, a few days later, enabled us to cause the arrest of the fugitive.

TESTING RETAIL BUSINESS ESTABLISHMENTS

The making of test purchases in retail stores is done very extensively, and for which work detectives are employed. Taking for example a high class confectionery store, drug store or cigar store. The proprietor may not come to his place of business until late in the morning, or may be away for perhaps a week. He desires to know if his sales clerks are honest and reliable, and courteous to customers during his absence from the place of business. The detective retained for this purpose enters the store one, two or three times a day and makes purchases the same as any other customer would, and while in the place makes careful note of the kind of treatment accorded him by the sales clerk, and in particular notes if the amount of his purchase is properly rung up on the cash register, with which most retail business establishments are now equipped. Owners of department stores and of saloons spend thousands of dollars annually for detective work of this kind.

DIVORCE CASES

As everyone knows, thousands of divorce actions are brought every year throughout the country and many detectives find employment in connection with such cases. The custom is that when the husband, for instance, suspects his wife of infidelity, he has her placed under surveillance for a month or so, which usually develops whether or not his suspicions are well founded. However, information and corroborative evidence is obtained by the husband, or by the wife, as the case may be, in a hundred other ways. While detective work of this nature has no doubt always been profitable to detectives, my opinion is that it has never been any too creditable, and my advice to the detective is to keep as clear of this kind of work as possible, because such cases require skillful work and handling, and often when handled successfully, the results do not offset the undesirable notoriety that may be given the detective.

ARSON

As is quite well known, the fire losses in the United States run annually into millions of dollars, and if one would take the trouble to have half an hour's talk with any fire insurance expert it will be found that a surprisingly large percentage of fires are no doubt the results of schemes to defraud fire insurance companies. Much detective work is directed in an effort to lessen these losses, and to bring about the arrest and conviction of the offenders, but my knowledge of conditions is that the crime of arson continues on the increase rather than on the decrease.

Life and accident insurance companies throughout the country employ hundreds of detectives the year round to investigate risks and fraudulent claims. Many individuals somewhere daily place in the hands of private detectives, various kinds of cases to be investigated, and in conclusion I will say that when a case is submitted to the detective for investigation it should be made the subject of careful thought and consideration. As a rule, every case differs in some way, but if good common sense methods are applied, results can be secured, no matter how difficult or how complicated the case may be at the start.

Milton Keynes UK
Ingram Content Group UK Ltd.
UKHW012237180624
444315UK00004B/447

9 789361 473296